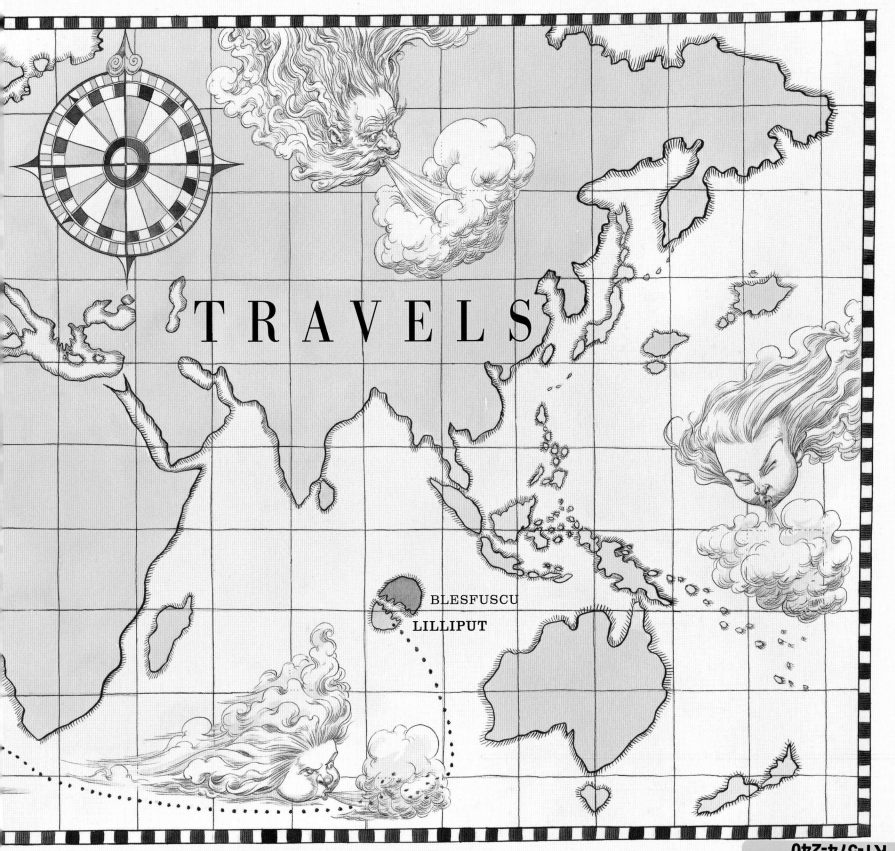

TRAVELS

BLESFUSCU
LILLIPUT

GULLIVER'S TRAVELS

retold by

MARTIN JENKINS

For my parents
M. J.

For my father
C.R.

First published 2004 in *Jonathan Swift's Gulliver* by Walker Books Ltd
87 Vauxhall Walk, London SE11 5HJ

2 4 6 8 10 9 7 5 3 1

Text © 2004 Martin Jenkins
Illustrations © 2004 Chris Riddell

The right of Martin Jenkins and Chris Riddell to be identified as author
and illustrator respectively of this work has been asserted by them in accordance
with the Copyright, Designs and Patents Act 1988

This book has been typeset in Clarendon T Light

Printed in Belgium

British Library Cataloguing in Publication Data:
a catalogue record for this book is available from the British Library

ISBN 978-1-4063-6865-9

www.walker.co.uk

G U L L _ _ _ _ _ AVELS

Voy_ _ _ _iput

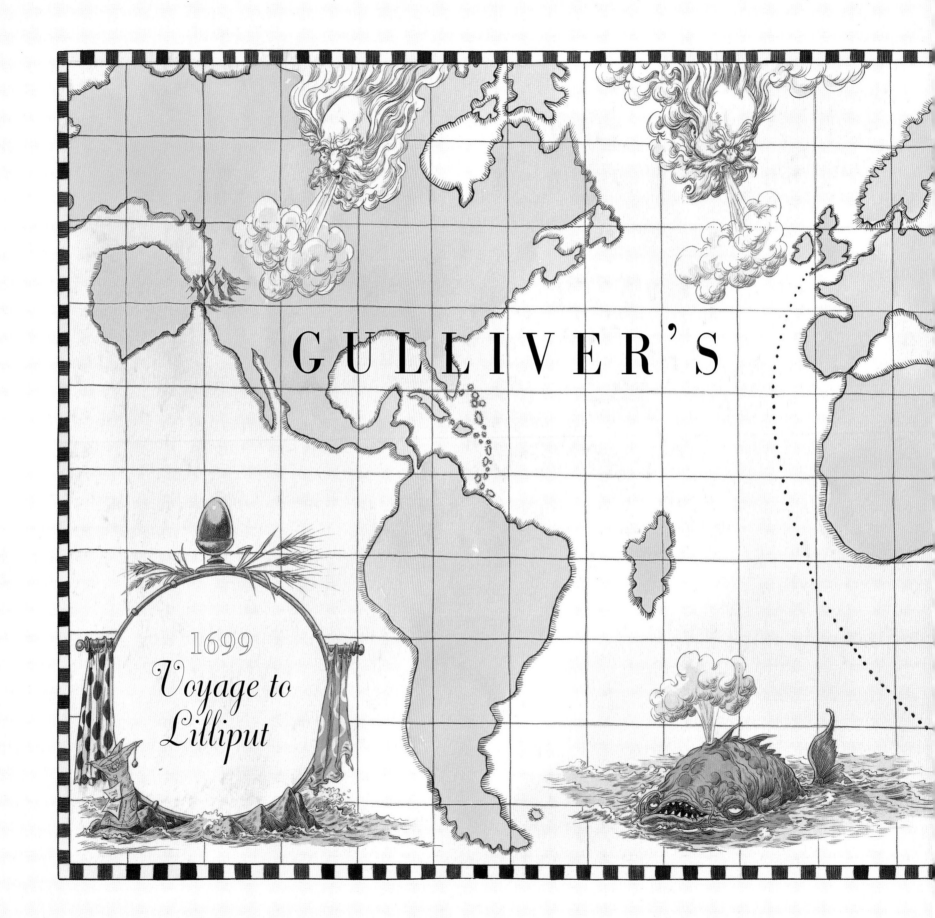

GULLIVER'S

1699
Voyage to
Lilliput

VOYAGE TO LILLIPUT

illustrated by

CHRIS RIDDELL

WALKER BOOKS
AND SUBSIDIARIES
LONDON • BOSTON • SYDNEY • AUCKLAND

$\mathcal{M}$y name is Lemuel Gulliver. I was born in Nottinghamshire and was sent to Cambridge University when I was fourteen years old. Three years later I began training as a surgeon, first in London and afterwards in Leyden, in the Netherlands. I made several voyages as a ship's surgeon, but grew tired of the sea and decided to set up as a doctor in Wapping, where I moved with my wife and children. However, business did not go well and I again took a post as a ship's surgeon.

The ship I was employed on, the *Antelope*, sailed from Bristol on 4 May 1699, bound for the South Seas. In early November, a violent storm blew the ship off course, and we ended up somewhere to the north-west of Tasmania. On 5 November the ship was driven onto a rock and wrecked. Six of us managed to escape in the lifeboat, but shortly afterwards it was overturned in a sudden gale. I swam as best I could and eventually found myself in shallow water within sight of land. I staggered ashore and, completely exhausted, fell asleep immediately.

When I awoke, it was just daylight. I was lying on my back and tried to sit up, only to find that I was stuck fast. I could not even move my head. It seemed that I was tied to the ground by hundreds of pieces of string.

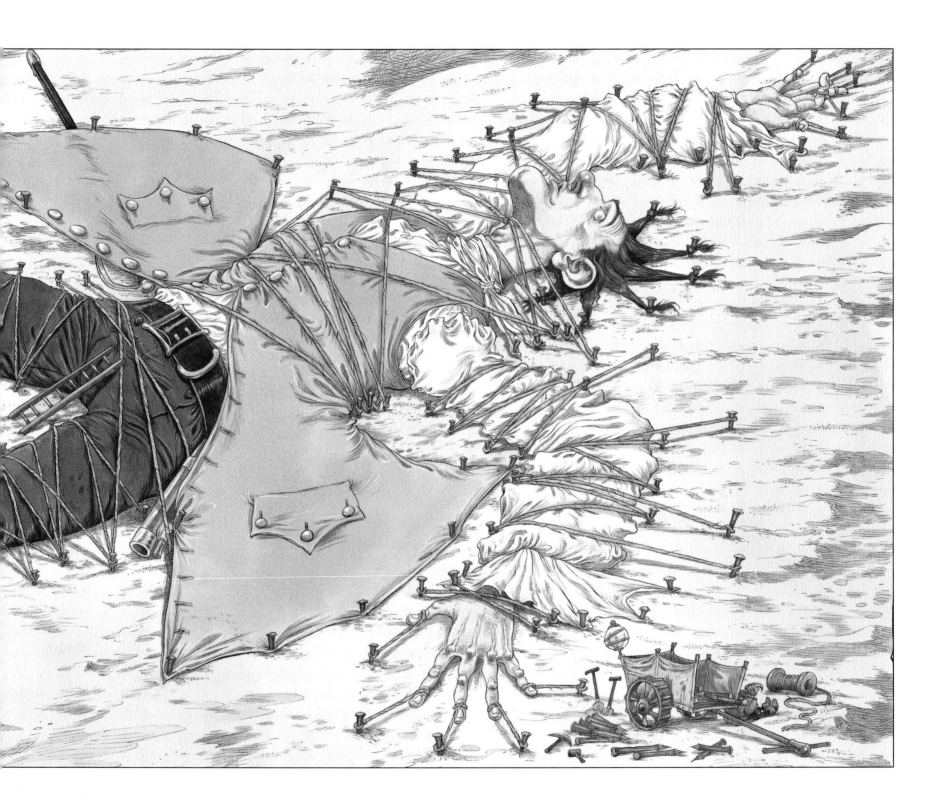

Eventually, as the sun was becoming uncomfortably bright and hot, I felt some living things moving up my left leg and onto my body, closely followed by about forty more. The first creature, whatever it was, came to a halt just under my chin, and by peering downwards I found I could just make it out. To my astonishment, what did I see but a miniature human no bigger than my hand, equipped with bow and arrow! In my amazement I let out a loud roar, and all the creatures turned and fled back down my body, some of them falling off in their hurry to get away. They were soon back, however.

Struggling to get loose, I finally managed to free my left arm, and, by pulling violently, loosened the threads tying my hair down, so that I could turn my head a little. I tried to grab a handful of the tiny men but they scurried off again, all yelling at once. Then one of

them cried, "Tolgo phonac" and I was instantly bombarded with hundreds of minute arrows, which pricked me like so many needles and hurt terribly. I quickly decided that it might be wise to lie still and try to free myself under cover of night, when I would be able to sneak away. Soon I heard a lot of clattering and banging to my right, and saw that a tall platform was being built. Four of the little creatures climbed up to it and the tallest of them, who seemed to be rather important, made a great long speech directed at me, of which I didn't understand a single word.

As you might imagine, I was absolutely starving by now and, although it was rather rude of me, I indicated this by pointing vigorously to my mouth. The important person understood immediately, and ordered food to be brought. It was all tiny — I ate three loaves of bread in one mouthful — but delicious. They then brought me wine to drink in what must have been their largest barrels, and some ointment to soothe the pain caused by the arrow wounds. They smeared my wounds with ointment and then loosed the ties on my left side — and not a moment too soon, for all the drink they had given me had filled my bladder to bursting. The creatures on my right side quickly realized what was going to happen and ran clear, turning to gasp in amazement at the gushing torrent I produced. I then gestured as best I could that I would like to be let free, trying to indicate that I would do them no harm, but they refused.

I soon fell deeply asleep (I later discovered that they had put a sleeping potion in the wine) and woke up to find something tickling my nostril, making me sneeze terribly. I found I was being carried on a sort of platform on wheels, drawn by no fewer than fifteen hundred horses.

We stopped near a large city, and my left ankle was bound with

chains to the front wall of a building that looked like some sort of temple. At least a hundred thousand people, including someone who was evidently the emperor himself, came out of the city to see me. Thousands of the sightseers clambered up ladders to swarm over my body, causing me considerable irritation, until the emperor forbade it.

When they were sure I was securely chained, my ropes were cut and I was at last able to stand up. You can imagine the commotion that caused. Feeling very down at heart, I turned round and crawled into the temple, where I found I could lie down at full stretch.

When I finally came out again, I found the emperor coming towards me on one of their miniature horses. He ordered me to be given food and drink, and began to speak to me. To see and hear him better, I lay down on my

side. He was very smartly dressed and much taller than the people around him, who included ladies in sumptuous dresses, and what appeared to be a number of priests and lawyers. The emperor, priests and lawyers spoke to me for over two hours and I replied in all the languages I could — I am very good at languages and know several — but they couldn't understand me and nor, for that matter, could I understand them.

The court then went off, leaving a large number of guards to keep the crowds away. Some ruffians were impertinent enough to shoot arrows at me as I sat on the ground outside my home. One of the arrows only narrowly missed my left eye. The man in charge of the guards seized six of the ringleaders and decided that the best way to punish them was to hand them over to me. I picked them up, put five of them in my coat pocket and then pretended to be about to eat the sixth. He was terrified, and let out an awful yell. I took out my pocket knife, which frightened them all even

more, but then used it to cut the ropes binding the man and put him gently on the ground. I then freed the other five in the same way. The soldiers and the crowd were very impressed by how merciful I had been.

As news of my arrival spread, huge numbers of people came to look at me. They all stopped work and the whole country threatened to grind to a halt. The emperor ordered everyone who had already seen me to go home, saying they could only come near me again if they paid a licence fee. The treasury made a lot of money collecting these fees.

In the meantime, I later learnt, the royal court were discussing what to do with me. They were afraid that I might break free, or eat all the country's food. They thought of starving me to death or poisoning me with their arrows, but then decided that my corpse would be too difficult to get rid of, and would soon start to rot and smell horrible, perhaps even causing a plague.

While the court were arguing, some soldiers came in and told them how kindly I had treated the criminals who had attacked me. The court were so impressed that they abandoned their plans to get rid of me, and instead decided I should be properly looked after. Each day I was to be fed six cows, forty sheep and lots of bread and wine, paid for by the treasury. Six hundred people were appointed to look after me; three hundred tailors were ordered to make me a suit; and six of the best teachers were to teach me the language. I soon started my lessons. The emperor himself often came to help. Each time, I begged him for my freedom, but he replied that I must be patient. In any case I would first have to swear an oath of peace and agree to be searched for any weapons.

With my consent, two of the emperor's agents searched me. Here is my translation of

Item Right waistcoat pocket: a bundle of thin white stuff, each piece about the size of three men, tied with cable and covered in black markings. We think this is his writing.

Item Left waistcoat pocket: an implement with numerous long poles sticking out. We think the Man Mountain combs his hair with this.

Item Large right-hand trouser pocket: a hollow pillar of iron, about the length of a man, attached to a huge piece of wood with more strangely shaped pieces of iron sticking out of the side.

their report:

Item Right coat pocket: a piece of coarse cloth the size of a carpet.

Item Left coat pocket: an enormous silver chest filled with dust that made us sneeze.

Item Large left-hand trouser pocket: another of same.

Item Small right-hand trouser pocket: several round flat pieces of red and silver metal.

Item Small left-hand trouser pocket: two irregularly shaped black pillars, each containing an enormous steel plate. The Man Mountain explained that one was for cutting his meat, the other for shaving his beard. In the top of his trousers were two tight pockets that we could not get into. He called them his fobs, and showed us what was in them.

In the right fob was a great silver chain, with a wonderful engine at one end, in the form of a globe, half silver and half transparent. On the transparent side were strange figures which we could not touch. The engine makes a noise like a watermill. We think it is either an unknown animal, or perhaps the Man Mountain's god. It is probably his god, as he told us he hardly ever did anything without consulting it first.

In the left fob was a net which contained several pieces of yellow metal. If these really are gold, they must be very valuable.

Around his waist was a great leather belt, from which hung a sword the length of five men and a pouch which contained several very heavy lumps of metal about the size of our heads and a heap of much smaller black grains.

Signed,

Clefren Frelock   Marsi Frelock

The emperor asked me to show him several of these things. He summoned three thousand soldiers to stand by, just to be on the safe side. I got out my sword, which flashed brightly in the sun, dazzling the soldiers and making them shout out in terror and surprise. Next I got out one of my pocket pistols and, putting some gunpowder in it, fired it into the air. As you might imagine, this terrified everyone even more than the sword, and hundreds of soldiers fell down in a dead faint.

At the emperor's order, I put these and all the other objects that Clefren and Marsi Frelock had found onto the ground. My sword, pistols and gunpowder pouch were taken to the emperor's stores, but everything else was given back to me.

I did not tell the emperor that I had another secret pocket. In it I had a pair of spectacles, a pocket telescope and other personal items, which I was afraid might become lost or broken if I revealed them.

By being as gentle and friendly as possible, I hoped to be allowed my freedom. The people quickly lost all fear of me, often coming to dance on my hand. The children would even play hide-and-seek in my hair.

One day the emperor entertained me with a show that was the most spectacular I have ever seen. The most impressive event was the rope-dancing. This is a sport carried out by people trying to gain important positions at court. When a post is vacant, because someone has died or has been disgraced (which happens pretty often), the candidates dance on the rope. Whoever jumps the highest wins. Chief ministers also often rope-dance, to show that they can still do it. The treasurer, Flimnap, is allowed to dance on a very high rope. My friend Reldresal, principal secretary for private affairs, dances just a bit lower. Often people fall off the ropes, breaking limbs or even killing themselves. A year or two ago Flimnap fell and would certainly have broken his neck if one of the emperor's cushions had not luckily been there to break his fall.

I learnt that the emperor, empress and first minister sometimes hold a private competition in the chamber of state. The emperor or his first minister holds out a stick which the competitors have to creep under or leap over. Whoever does this the longest gets a blue piece of silk. The runner-up gets a red piece and the person who comes third a green one. All these are worn proudly at court. I decided to organize some games of my own. I took some tree-trunks and my handkerchief and made a sort of arena on which twenty-four horses and their riders

carried out lots of complicated manoeuvres, including fighting mock battles. It was all very exciting. Unfortunately one of the horses put its foot through my handkerchief, throwing its rider. The rider was fine but the horse hurt its shoulder and I decided not to risk any more games like this.

A couple of days after this the emperor was inspecting his troops and decided that it would be amusing to have them march between my legs. There were three thousand soldiers on foot and a thousand on horse-back. The soldiers were all forbidden from looking up — my trousers were in a very tattered state by now. Some of them sneaked a look though, and I distinctly heard their guffaws and titters.

At last my pleas for freedom were heard in the council. Only one person opposed it – the chief admiral, or galbet, whose name was Skyresh Bolgolam and who had decided that he was my enemy. Even he was finally persuaded; I had to swear an oath and agree to obey the commands in the following proclamation:

"Golbasto Momaren Evlame Gurdilo Shefin Mully Ully Gue, most Mighty Emperor of Lilliput, Delight and Terror of the Universe, etc. etc., taller than the sons of men, etc. etc., proposeth to the Man Mountain that he shall:

☛ not leave our kingdom without permission;

☛ only enter the capital with our permission, and with two hours' warning to allow everyone to get out of his way;

☛ confine his walks to our main roads, and not lie down in any fields;

☛ be very careful not to squash people,

horses or carriages when walking, and only pick someone up with their permission;

☛ if needed, carry a royal messenger across the country once a month;

☛ be our ally against our enemies on the island of Blefuscu and do his best to destroy their fleet, which is preparing to invade us;

☛ when at his leisure, help our workmen to build walls in the royal park and elsewhere;

☛ tell us how big our kingdom is by walking round the coast and counting his steps.

If he agrees to all this, he will be provided with enough food and drink each day to feed 1,728 of our subjects." (A friend at court explained that they had reached this figure by calculating that because I was twelve times taller than them, my body would contain twelve times twelve times twelve of theirs, and would need that times as much food to keep going.)

I of course agreed to all these conditions, although I wasn't totally happy with some of them (which had been added by my enemy Skyresh Bolgolam).

The first thing I did with my new-found freedom was tour the capital, Mildendo. I walked very carefully, in case anyone should still be outdoors. I couldn't reach the emperor's palace as the buildings of the courtyards around it were too high for me to step over, and I thought I might damage them if I climbed on them.

To overcome this I spent the next three days in the royal park outside the city, cutting down some of the largest trees. With these I made a pair of stools which I then used to step over the buildings. I lay down in the courtyard to look inside the royal apartments, which were magnificent. The empress was kind enough to hold her hand out of the window for me to kiss.

About a fortnight after I had been set free, Reldresal came to see me in

private. He explained that all was not well in Lilliput. There were two groups at court, the Tramecksan and the Slamecksan, who hated each other. The Tramecksan wore high-heeled shoes, the Slamecksan low-heeled ones. The present emperor favoured the Slamecksan and wore lower heels than anyone else. His son, however, the heir to the throne, wore one heel higher than the other (which made him hobble), indicating that he leant a little towards the Tramecksan.

The two groups were always plotting against each other. To make matters worse, the country had been at war for thirty-six months with the neighbouring country of Blefuscu. The cause of the war had been eggs.

Originally, everyone in Lilliput and Blefuscu had opened their eggs at the larg-

er end. But the current emperor's grandfather had cut his finger as a boy when breaking open an egg at the big end. Because of this his

father, the emperor at the time, ordered everyone to open their eggs at the smaller end. The population resented this terribly; one emperor lost his life, and another was deposed in the ensuing troubles. Eleven thousand people were thought to have been killed rather than agree to break their eggs at the smaller end.

Many others fled to Blefuscu. Big-endian books were banned and big-endians prevented from having jobs.

The emperor of Blefuscu even accused the Lilliputian emperor of creating a division in the religion, by going against the great Prophet Lustrog in the Brundrecal, their holy book. Lustrog stated that: "all true Believers shall break their Eggs at the convenient End." According to the Blefuscudian emperor (and all the other big-endians), this was obviously the large end.

The big-endian Lilliputians who had fled to Blefuscu finally persuaded the emperor there to wage war on Lilliput. So far the Lilliputians had lost thirty thousand soldiers and sailors in the war, along with forty large ships and countless smaller ones. Blefuscu had lost even more, but had managed to assemble a big fleet and was preparing to invade Lilliput.

The emperor had sent Reldresal to ask for my help. Although as a foreigner I felt I should not interfere in the arguments of the Lilliputians, I was prepared to defend the emperor and his country against invaders.

The island of Blefuscu lay around eight hundred metres off the north-east coast of Lilliput. No contact was allowed between the two islands and I had avoided that side of Lilliput, so that no Blefuscudian could have seen me, or had any idea that I existed.

I hatched a bold plan to capture their fleet. I asked for a large number of the strongest ropes and heaviest iron bars to be brought to me. The ropes were like thin string and the bars about as thick as knitting needles.

I twisted the bars together in threes and

bent the ends to form hooks. I then tied lengths of rope, also twisted in threes, to the hooks and, carrying these, set off for the channel separating Lilliput from Blefuscu. Just before high tide I waded out. I had to swim across the deeper middle part, but within half an hour I was approaching Blefuscu. The enemy sailors were so frightened when they saw me that they all jumped into the water and swam for their lives. They then gathered in a great group back on shore; there must have been about thirty thousand of them.

Having reached the deserted ships, I started to fix a hook to each one, gathering the ropes attached to the hooks in a great bundle as I went along. The Blefuscudians tried to stop me by bombarding me with arrows, which stung terribly. My main fear was that they would hit me in the eyes and blind me. Then I remembered the pair of glasses hidden in my secret pocket. I fixed these firmly on my nose and was able to continue with my plan.

As soon as I had hooked up all the ships, I

gave a great heave and ... nothing moved! The ships were still anchored fast, so I dropped the ropes and, getting out my knife, quickly cut through all the anchor chains. Then off I set back for Lilliput, pulling fifty of their largest ships behind me. When the Blefuscudians saw what I was doing, they let out a deafening scream of grief and despair. As soon as I was out of range, I stopped to pick out the arrows that had stuck into me, and rubbed in some of the soothing ointment that had been given to me when I first arrived in Lilliput. I waited for the tide to drop a little and continued on.

The Lilliputians first saw the fleet approaching when it was in the middle of the channel. They could not see me because I was up to my neck in water. They were convinced that I had drowned and that the enemy was sailing over to attack them.

They were about to despair, when they spotted me. They let out a great cry of triumph and as soon as I reached shore, the emperor made me a nardac, which is the highest honour in the country.

The emperor was overjoyed at the victory, and asked me to go back and capture the rest of the Blefuscudian ships. He decided that he wanted to conquer Blefuscu and turn it into a province of Lilliput. Everybody would be forced to break their eggs at the small end, and as far as he was concerned he would be emperor of the whole world. I tried to dissuade him from his plan, saying I didn't want to play any part in turning a brave people like the Blefuscudians into slaves.

Many government ministers agreed with me. However, the emperor never forgave me for opposing him, and, as I was soon to discover, began plotting against me with several of his ministers.

About three weeks after I had captured the ships, ambassadors arrived from Blefuscu with an offer of peace. I helped them a little in the negotiations, and when a peace treaty had finally been signed, the ambassadors paid me a visit. They invited me in turn to visit the emperor of Blefuscu.

During my next audience with the emperor of Lilliput I asked his permission to travel to Blefuscu. He agreed, but in a very cold way. I did not understand why the emperor was being so unfriendly, but I later learnt that Flimnap and Bolgolam had persuaded him that I had been plotting against him with the Blefuscudian ambassadors. I began to realize how treacherous courts and ministers could be.

About this time, I had a chance to do a great favour for the emperor – at least I thought so at the time. One night I was woken by hundreds of people shouting at my door. Some court officials explained that the empress's rooms in the royal palace had caught fire. I rushed to the palace. The Lilliputians were already trying to put the fire out with buckets of water, but these were proving useless. I could have smothered the flames with my coat, but had left it in my house.

The fire was spreading and it looked as if the whole palace was going to burn to the ground, when suddenly I had an idea. That evening I had drunk a huge amount of a very tasty kind of wine called glimigrim, so I had a very full bladder. I quickly relieved myself in the direction of the empress's apartment and was able to put the fire out in three minutes.

Having done so, I immediately went back home. I knew it was strictly against

the law for anyone to make water within the palace walls, but hoped the emperor would understand my reasons and forgive me. I heard that he did order the chief court to issue me a pardon, but I never received it. What's more, the empress was apparently so disgusted with what I had done that she refused ever again to use the rooms where the fire had broken out. And she too began plotting against me.

Before I go on recounting my adventures, I should describe some of the more interesting things about the Lilliputians and their country.

They write diagonally on a page, from one corner to the opposite.

They bury their dead with their heads pointing downwards. They do this because they believe that in eleven thousand months all the dead will come back to life. At this time the earth, which they think is flat, will turn upside down, which means that the dead will find themselves back on their feet. (Actually, highly educated Lilliputians think this is nonsense, but many other people still believe it.)

They think that deceiving people is a worse crime than stealing. Being ungrateful is punishable by death. If someone accuses another person of committing a crime against the government and the accused person is found innocent, the accuser is immediately put to death. The person accused is paid compensation from the property of the accuser and their innocence is proclaimed everywhere.

If anyone can prove that they have faithfully obeyed all the laws of the country for a period of seventy-three months, they are rewarded with money from a special fund and are allowed to add the word snilpall, which means 'legal', to their name.

The Lilliputians' ideas about parents and children are very different from ours. They do not think that children should be grateful to

Upper-class boys are sent to schools staffed by very distinguished teachers. The boys' food and clothes are very plain and simple. They are dressed by men until they are four years old, after which time they dress themselves, however important their family might be. They are always kept busy, except when they are eating and sleeping, and have two hours of physical exercise a day. They are

their parents for having been born, and they think that parents are quite the worst people to educate their own children. Because of this, when they are twenty months old, all children except those of the poorest working people are sent to public nurseries or schools. There are separate schools for boys and girls, and for different classes of children.

brought up to be honourable, just, courageous, modest, merciful, religious and patriotic. They never talk to servants, and their parents are only allowed to see them twice a year, each time for only an hour and always with a teacher in attendance. The parents are allowed to kiss the children when they arrive and leave, but are not allowed to bring any presents, or speak fondly or whisper to them. The children are kept at school until they are fifteen years old (which is equivalent to our twenty-one), but are given more and more freedom in the last three years.

Middle-class boys have a similar upbringing, while working-class boys are sent out to learn a trade when they are seven.

Upper-class girls are treated very much like the boys, except that they are dressed by female servants, always in the presence of a teacher, until they are five years old, when they start to dress themselves. If any servant is ever found to have tried to entertain the girls by telling frightening or silly stories, she is publicly whipped, locked up in prison for a year and then banished to the most distant part of Lilliput. The girls' education is similar to that of the boys, except that their physical exercises are a little less strenuous and they are taught fewer subjects, although they are given lessons in how to run a home. They are considered old enough to get married when they are twelve years old, at which time they are taken away from the school by their parents or guardians. As with boys, working-class girls leave school at seven.

The care and education of the children is paid for by their parents. The poorest labourers, who tend the country's farms and grow crops, are not educated as children, but they are looked after in homes when they are old or ill.

Because of this there is no begging in Lilliput.

I will now give a short account of my own life there.

Being good with my hands, I made a table and chair out of the largest trees in the royal park. Two hundred seamstresses were employed to make my shirts, bedlinen and tablecloths. Three hundred tailors made the rest of my clothes, and three hundred cooks, who lived with their families in huts around my house, prepared my food. I would put twenty waiters on the table to serve my meals, while a hundred more waited on the ground below. Their mutton wasn't quite as good as ours, but their beef was excellent.

One day the emperor decided that he and his family would like to come and dine with me. They sat on chairs on my table, with their guards standing in attendance. Flimnap the treasurer was there too, looking very sour. I

ate more than usual, to impress the emperor. I learnt later that this had given Flimnap another chance to attack me, for he persuaded the emperor that looking after me was bankrupting the country. He said that I had already cost the treasury over one and a half million sprugs (their most valuable gold coin) and that the emperor should get rid of me as soon as possible.

While I am talking about the treasurer, I must take the chance to stamp out some evil gossip. It has been said that the treasurer's wife took something of a fancy to me, and even visited me alone, in secret. This is absolute nonsense. She certainly came to visit quite often, but always with other people – usually her sister and daughter and a friend. But then many people would visit me. I used to put them in their coaches on a table with a rim around it. The coaches – often there would be as many as four at once – would drive in a circle

while I chatted to the people riding in them.

Although Flimnap was finally persuaded that the stories were untrue, he continued to turn the emperor more and more against me.

About this time I had a secret visit from an important person in court. I had done him a great favour at a time when he had been very unpopular with the emperor, and I knew that I could trust him.

He told me that several powerful people had prepared a document accusing me of high treason. They were Skyresh Bolgolam, the admiral, who had always been my enemy and hated me even more after my victory over the Blefuscudians; Flimnap, the treasurer; Limtoc, the general; Lalcon, the chamberlain; and Balmuff, the chief judge.

The document accused me of committing many crimes, of which the following were the most important:

1. I had relieved myself in the royal palace.

2. Having captured the Blefuscudian fleet, I had refused to help the emperor conquer Blefuscu and turn it into a province of Lilliput.

3. I had helped the Blefuscudian ambassadors.

4. I had asked to visit Blefuscu, and, having had only spoken agreement from the emperor, intended to carry out the visit.

My informant told me that while the document was being discussed, the emperor had several times defended me, reminding the others of the various ways in which I had helped him. But the treasurer and the admiral would have none of it. They insisted that my house be set on fire at night, so that I burnt horribly to death, while the general was to send twenty thousand men to fire poisoned arrows into my face and hands. At the same time, servants were to be ordered to smear my shirts and sheets with a burning poison that would make me die in agony. The general was persuaded to agree with them, but the emperor still thought that my life should be spared. He asked Reldresal, my friend, for his advice. Reldresal suggested that blinding me would be a severe enough punishment for my crimes.

Bolgolam, the admiral, was outraged. He accused me of being a secret big-ender, and maintained that this was quite enough reason for me to be killed.

The treasurer agreed, and pointed out that just blinding me would not solve the problem of the expense of keeping me. Indeed, I might eat even more when I was blind.

The emperor agreed that blinding me might not be a severe enough punishment, but he still didn't want to have me executed. At this point Reldresal suggested that I could be fed a smaller and smaller amount each day so that I would gradually weaken and eventually die of starvation. In that way, when I died there would be much less of me to rot and smell.

Everyone finally agreed to this, although the plan of starving me to death was to be kept a secret. The operation to blind me was to take place in three days' time.

Having heard all this I had to work out what to do. I thought of resisting – I could have easily smashed the capital city to pieces with rocks – but decided that this went against my honour as a nardac. Instead I decided to go to Blefuscu, as the emperor had given me permission to do.

The next morning I set off for the coast and seized a large man-of-war from the Lilliputian fleet. Taking off my clothes, I put these into the ship, along with my bedspread, and crossed the strait to the royal port of Blefuscu. The people there had been expecting my arrival for some time. They lent me two guides to show me the way to the capital, also called Blefuscu. The emperor and empress of Blefuscu came out of the city to greet me. I did not tell them of my disgrace, but said I had come to visit as I had promised I would, with the emperor of Lilliput's permission.

The emperor and his court treated me extremely well, although there was no building large enough to house me so I had a very

uncomfortable time sleeping on the ground wrapped in my bedspread.

Three days after my arrival I was walking round the north-east coast of Blefuscu, when I spotted what seemed to be an overturned boat out at sea. I pulled off my shoes and stockings and waded out towards it. It was indeed a real boat, which was being driven to the shore by the tide. I immediately returned to the capital and asked the emperor to lend me twenty of the tallest ships he had left after the loss of his fleet, along with three thousand sailors. The ships sailed round the coast while I returned across the island. I stripped off and made for the boat. I tied the front of the boat to one of the Blefuscudian ships, and swam, pushing the boat with one hand and taking a lot of rests, until the water was shallow enough for me to stand in. I then attached ropes to nine more ships and with these pulling and me pushing we got the boat close to shore. I waited for the tide to go out and then, with the help of two thousand men and many ropes and ingenious

machines, managed to right the boat, which turned out to be quite undamaged.

I took ten days to make a pair of paddles and then rowed the boat round the island to the royal port. The people there were amazed at the sight of it. I explained to the emperor that this was a chance for me to return to my own country, and asked his permission to equip the boat and leave Blefuscu. He kindly agreed.

I had been expecting to hear something from the emperor of Lilliput by now. I later learnt that he had not realized I knew what he was planning to do to me, and thought I had simply gone to Blefuscu to pay a visit and would soon return. I was away for such a long time that he became suspicious and sent an important person to Blefuscu with a copy of the document setting out my crimes. The person explained that I was fleeing from justice and if I did not return in two hours I would have the title of nardac taken away from me and would be declared a traitor. The emperor of Blefuscu would then be expected to tie me hand and foot and send me back to Lilliput.

The emperor of Blefuscu thought this over for three days and sent a message back to Lilliput saying that, although I had taken the Blefuscudian fleet, I had been very helpful to them when the peace treaty was being agreed. He could not therefore treat me like a criminal. However, he added, I had found an enormous boat, big enough to carry me away, so in a few weeks both empires would be rid of me.

The emperor of Blefuscu told me all this, and added in private that I would be protected by him if I would stay and serve Blefuscu. I decided that I didn't really trust emperors and ministers very much any more, and said that, although this was very kind of him, I would prefer to try to get home. I gathered afterwards that the emperor and his ministers were all rather relieved at this.

I got the boat together as quickly as I could. Five hundred workmen made me a pair of sails, and the emperor's carpenters helped me make oars and masts. A month later I was ready to depart. The emperor and his family came to bid me goodbye. I lay down to kiss their hands and His Majesty presented me with his full-length portrait along with fifty purses each containing two hundred sprugs. I stored the carcasses of a hundred oxen and three hundred sheep on board, together with six live cows, two bulls, six ewes and two rams, as well as plenty of hay and corn. I would happily have taken a number of Blefuscudians, but the emperor wouldn't permit it. He had my pockets thoroughly searched and made me promise not to carry anyone off, even if they wished to go with me.

I set sail at 6 a.m. on 24 September 1701. That night I found a small uninhabited island, where I cast anchor. I woke two hours before sunrise and set off again, heading north-west. The day after, I saw a ship in the distance. I caught up with it that evening and found to my delight that it was an English merchant ship, returning home from Japan. The captain, Mr John Biddel of Deptford, was an excellent fellow and a very good sailor.

Among the crew was an old friend of mine, Peter Williams, who assured the captain that I was trustworthy. The captain asked where I had come from and I explained as best I could. At first he thought me completely mad, but then I brought out my sheep and cattle, which convinced him that I was telling the truth. I showed him the portrait of the emperor of Blefuscu and some other souvenirs and gave him two of the purses of sprugs. I also promised him a pregnant cow and sheep once we arrived in England.

We reached England on 13 April, 1702. The only misfortune on the voyage was the loss of one of my sheep, carried off by rats. The rest of the sheep and cows I put out to pasture on a bowling green at Greenwich.

I spent the next two months with my wife and children and started to write an account of my travels, but then became desperate to see more countries. I made sure my family would be well provided for and then, in June 1702, I set off for the Downs to look for a ship that would take me on another voyage of adventure.

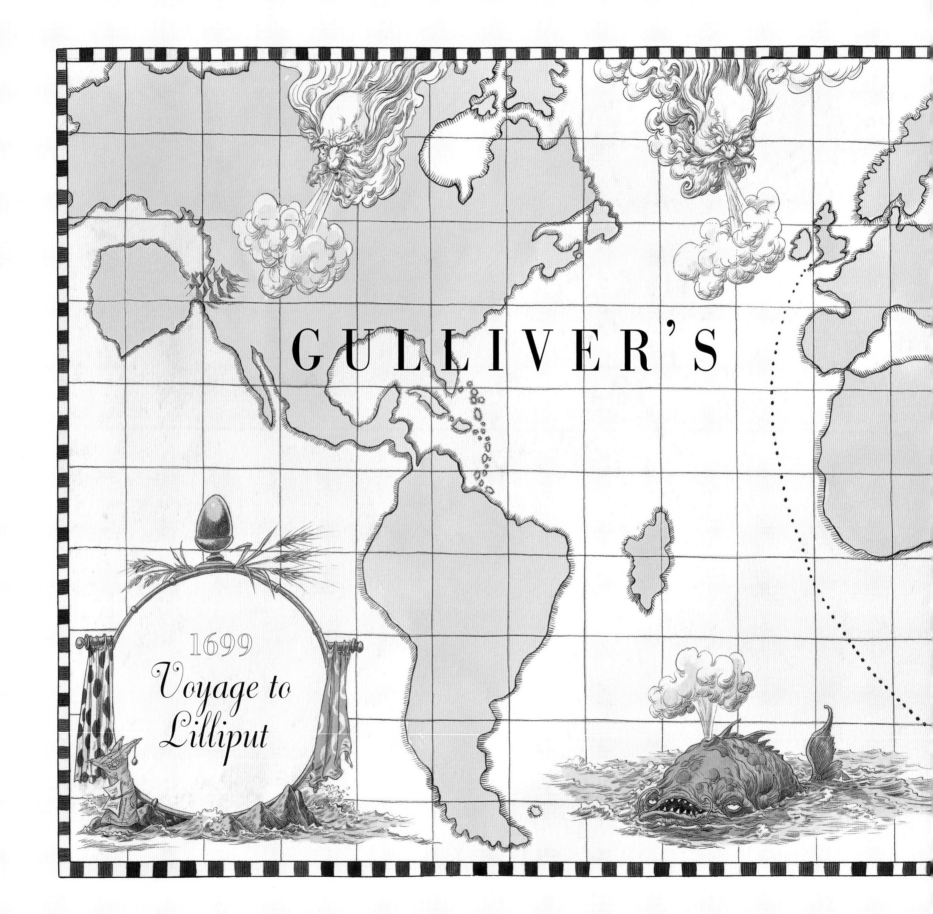

GULLIVER'S

1699
*Voyage to
Lilliput*

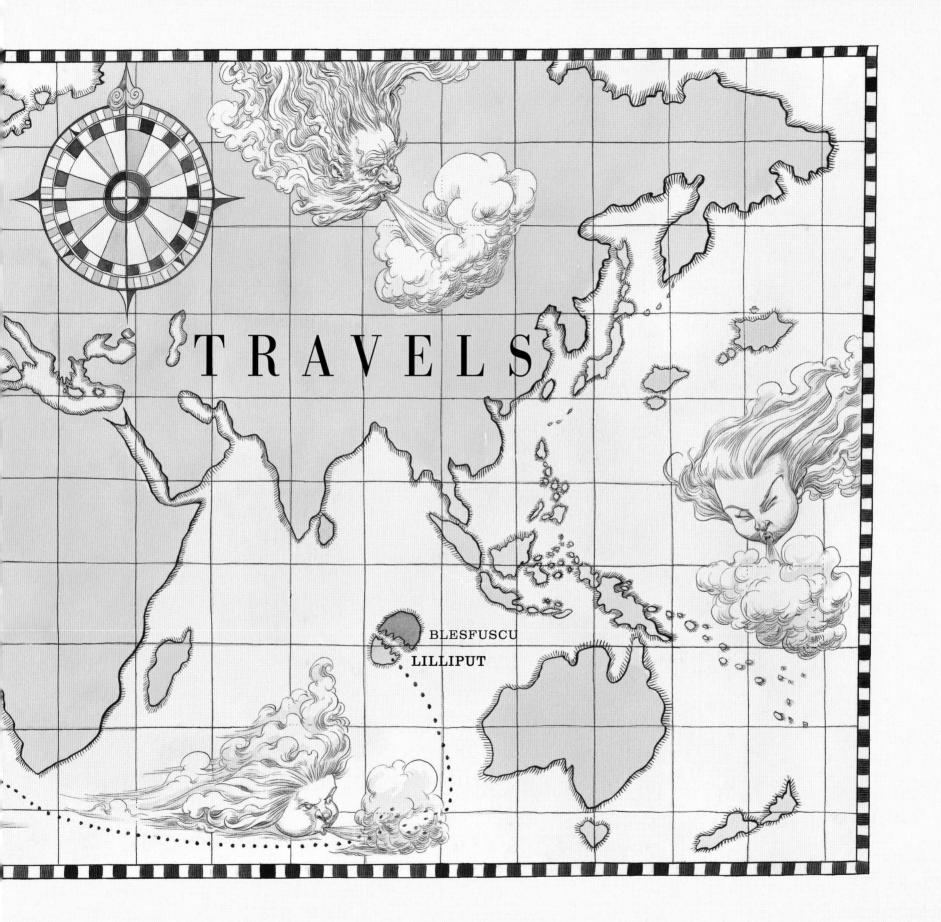

Read all of Gulliver's adventures in:

978-1-4063-0174-8

Winner of the Kate Greenaway Medal

"Deliciously quirky, savagely entertaining."
The Times

"Every page a cornucopia of imagination and wit. Should be presented to every child."
The Independent

"Teeming with absurd detail that Gulliver himself would have appreciated."
The Guardian